Puzzle Maps U.S.A.

Puzzle Maps U.S.A.

Nancy L. Clouse

Henry Holt and Company · New York

In memory of Mary Jane Anway—
artist, educator, and friend

Published by Henry Holt and Company, Inc.,
115 West 18th Street, New York, New York 10011.
Published in Canada by Fitzhenry & Whiteside Limited,
195 Allstate Parkway, Markham, Ontario L3R 4T8.

Library of Congress Cataloging-in-Publication Data
Clouse, Nancy L.
   Puzzle maps U.S.A. / Nancy L. Clouse
   Summary: Introduces the fifty states and their shapes through a
series of simple puzzle maps.
   ISBN 0-8050-1143-9
   1. United States—Geography—Juvenile literature.   2. United
States—Maps—Juvenile literature.   3. Children's questions
and answers.   4. Puzzles—Juvenile literature.   [1. United States—
Maps.   2. Puzzles.]   I. Title.
E161.3.C46   1990
912.73—dc20   89-24604

Henry Holt books are available at special discounts
for bulk purchases for sales promotions, premiums,
fund-raising, or educational use. Special editions
or book excerpts can also be created to specification.

   For details contact:

   Special Sales Director
   Henry Holt and Company, Inc.
   115 West 18th Street
   New York, New York 10011

First Edition
Printed in the United States of America
10 9 8 7 6 5 4 3 2 1

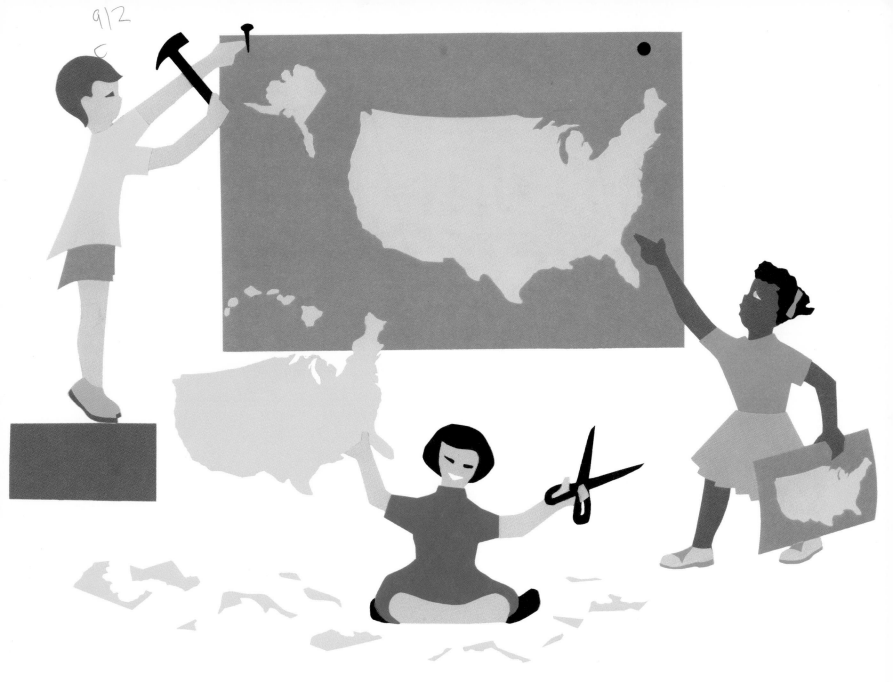

Maps can be a lot of fun!

Alaska*

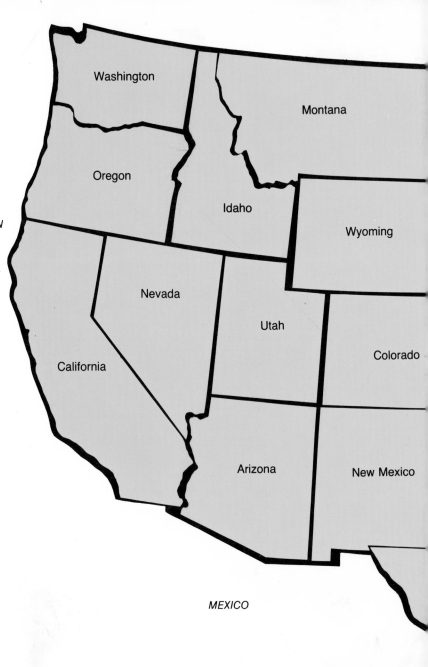

PACIFIC OCEAN

Washington

Montana

Oregon

Idaho

Wyoming

Nevada

Utah

Colorado

California

Arizona

New Mexico

MEXICO

Here is a map of the United States.

There are 50 states in all.
Can you find the state where you live?

Hawaii*

*Not to scale

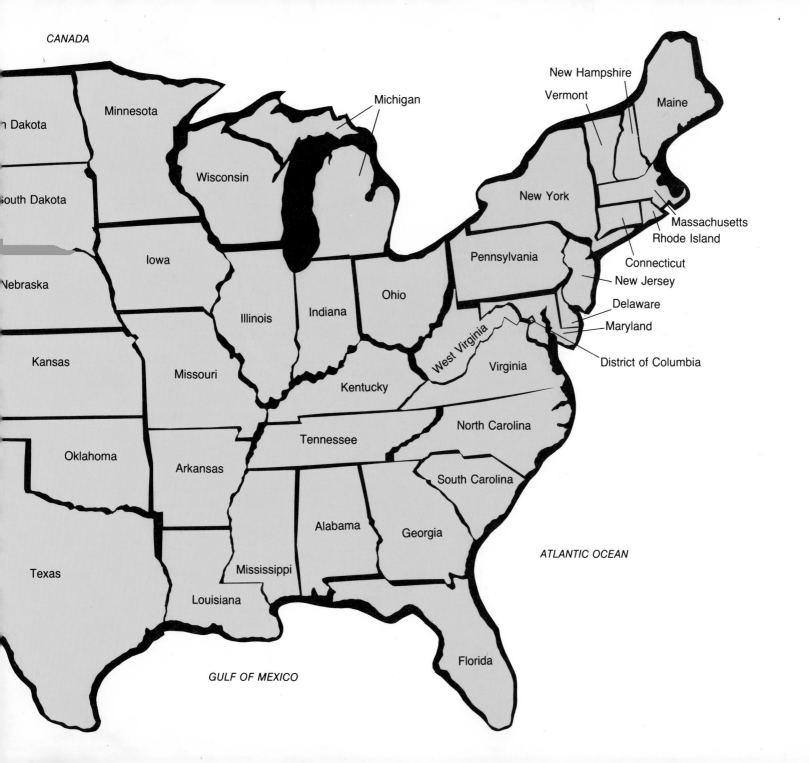

CANADA

Minnesota

h Dakota

South Dakota

Nebraska

Kansas

Oklahoma

Texas

Wisconsin

Michigan

Iowa

Illinois

Indiana

Ohio

Missouri

Kentucky

Arkansas

Tennessee

Mississippi

Louisiana

Alabama

Georgia

Florida

West Virginia

Virginia

North Carolina

South Carolina

New Hampshire

Vermont

Maine

New York

Pennsylvania

Massachusetts

Rhode Island

Connecticut

New Jersey

Delaware

Maryland

District of Columbia

ATLANTIC OCEAN

GULF OF MEXICO

7

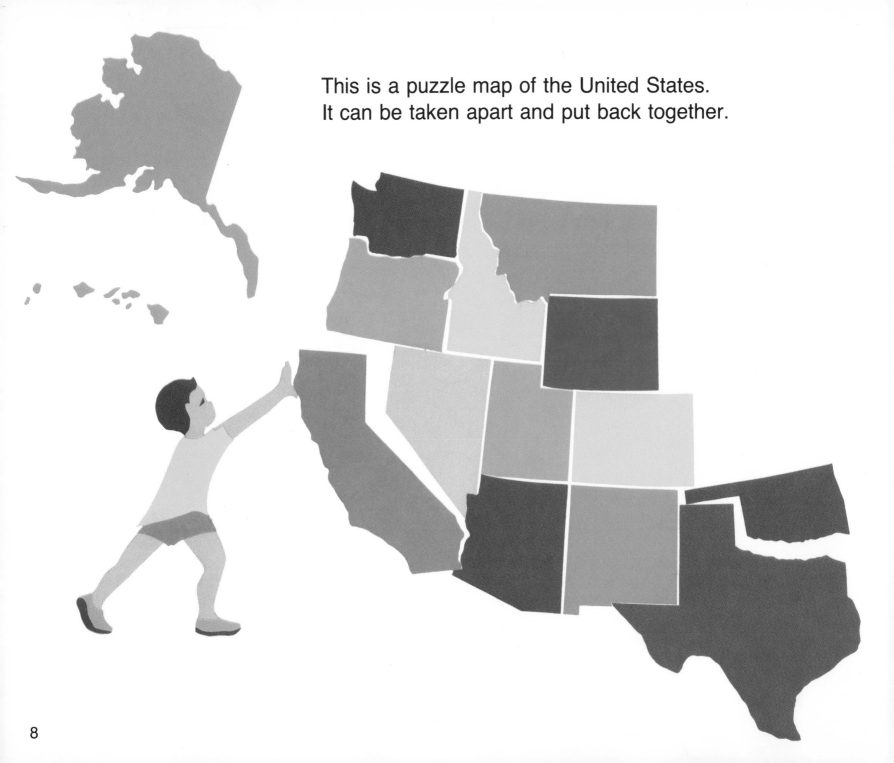

This is a puzzle map of the United States.
It can be taken apart and put back together.

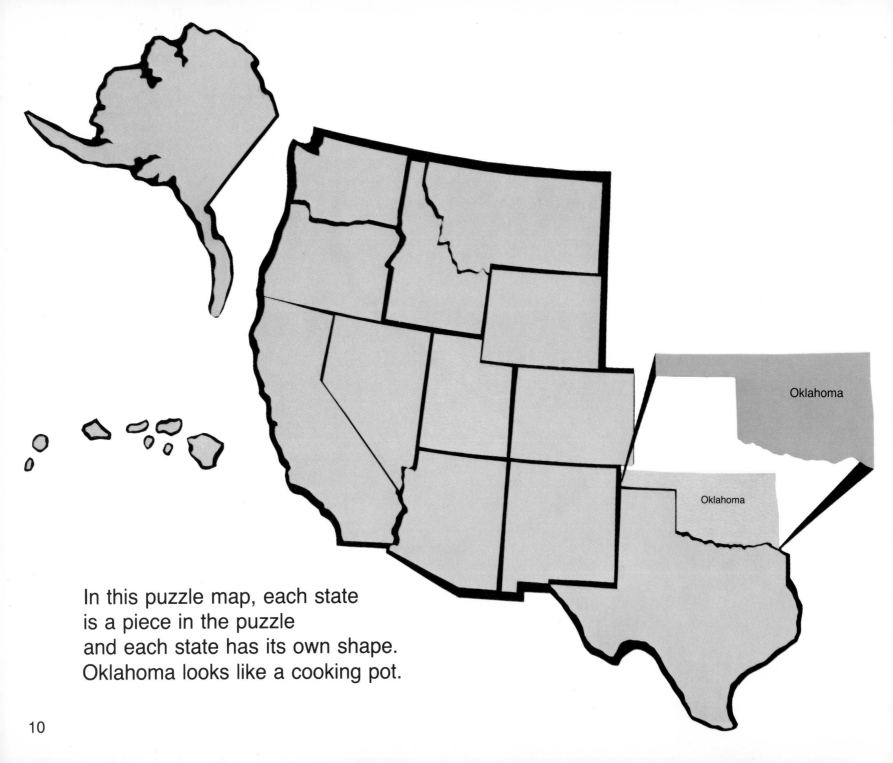

Oklahoma

Oklahoma

In this puzzle map, each state
is a piece in the puzzle
and each state has its own shape.
Oklahoma looks like a cooking pot.

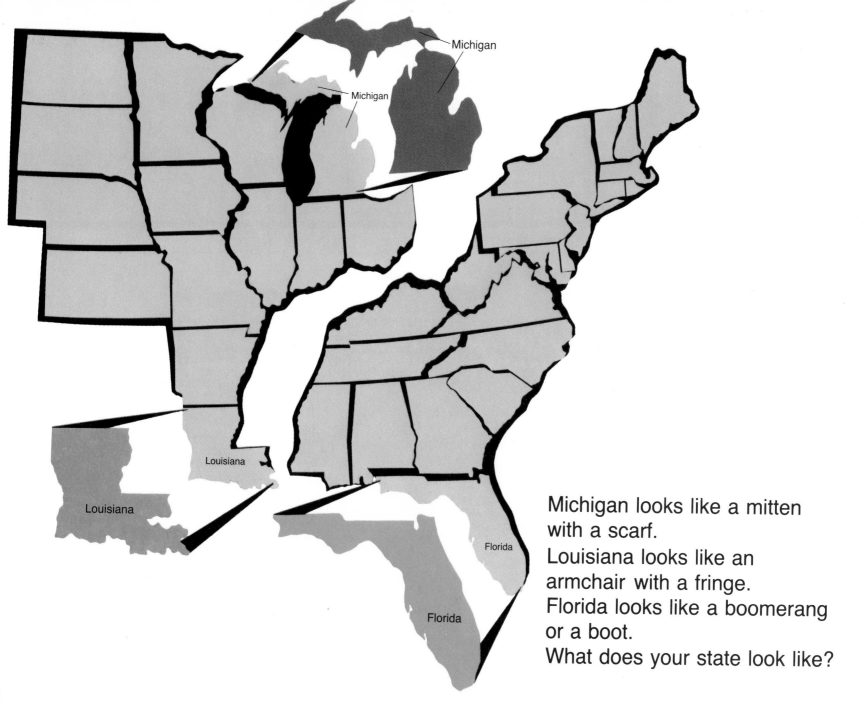

Michigan

Michigan

Louisiana

Louisiana

Florida

Florida

Michigan looks like a mitten with a scarf.

Louisiana looks like an armchair with a fringe.

Florida looks like a boomerang or a boot.

What does your state look like?

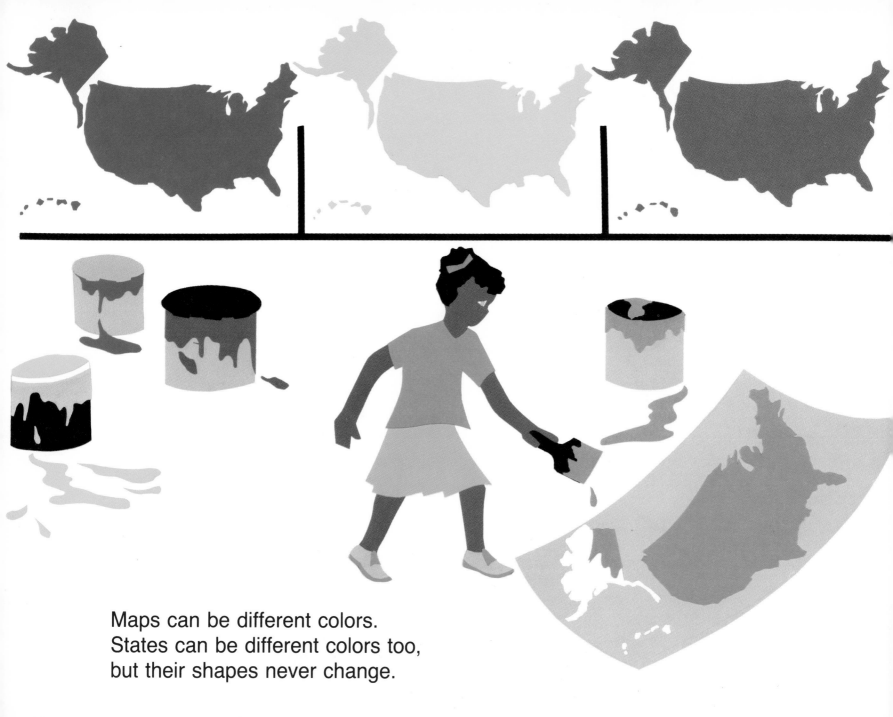

Maps can be different colors.
States can be different colors too,
but their shapes never change.

There are ten puzzle pieces on this page, but only three states.
Colorado looks like a box. How many times do you see Colorado?
California looks like an arm bent at the elbow. How many times
do you see California?
South Carolina looks like a funny triangle. How many times
do you see South Carolina?

13

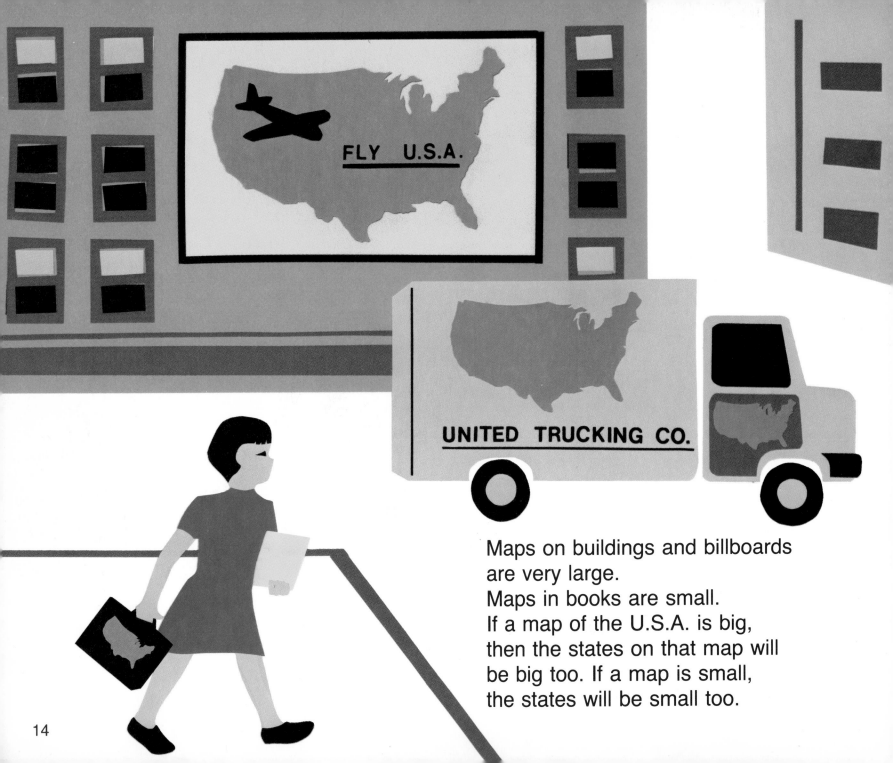

FLY U.S.A.

UNITED TRUCKING CO.

Maps on buildings and billboards
are very large.
Maps in books are small.
If a map of the U.S.A. is big,
then the states on that map will
be big too. If a map is small,
the states will be small too.

14

In this picture some states are big and some are small.
Is your state one of the kites flying high in the sky?

Maine, Nevada, New Mexico

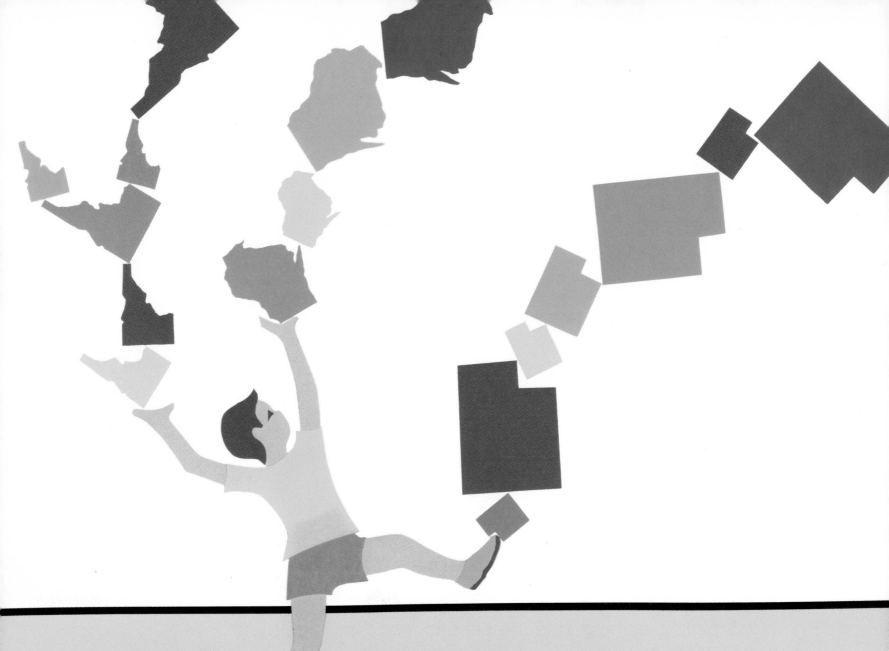

These puzzle shapes are hard to juggle,

16

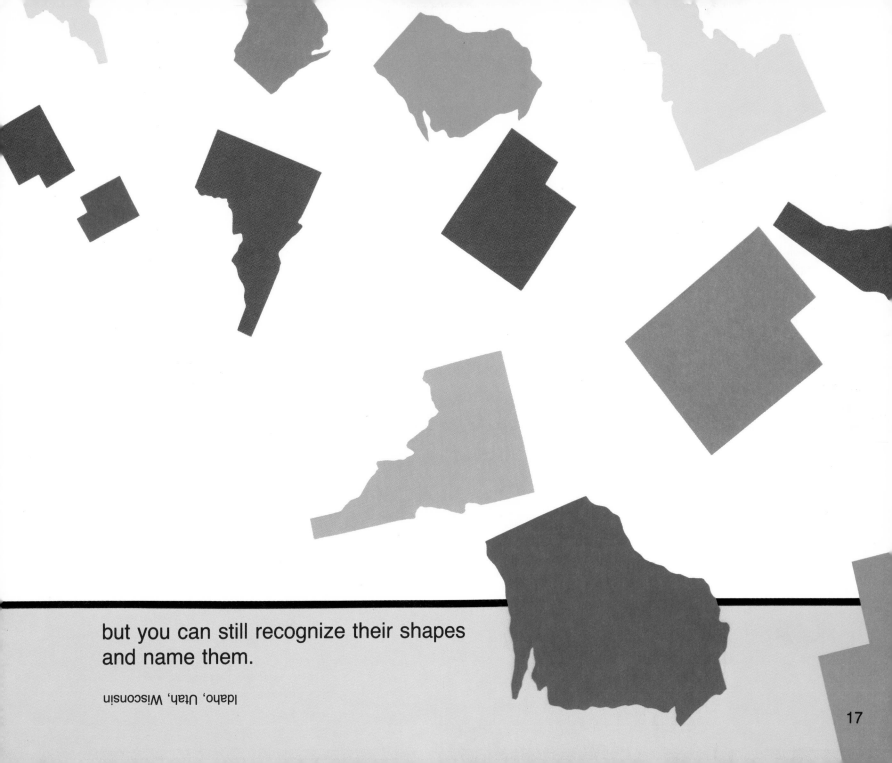

but you can still recognize their shapes
and name them.

Idaho, Utah, Wisconsin

17

Here's a picture-puzzle wagon. When you pull it,
Utah, Kansas, New Mexico, and Oklahoma go for a ride.

This turtle is going for a swim. Which states are going to get wet? The turtle's eye is the smallest state in the United States. Look closely at the turtle and you will find eight states in all.

Alabama, Connecticut, Kansas, Kentucky, Missouri, Nebraska, Oklahoma, Rhode Island

This funny bird wishes he could fly. Virginia and North Carolina are hiding in his bill. How many other states are in his feathers?

Alaska, Connecticut, Indiana, Kentucky, North Carolina, South Carolina, Texas, Virginia, West Virginia

This is a tree you'd never find in the park. Its trunk is made from Georgia, Mississippi, and Alabama. Which states are in the leaves?

Alabama, Florida, Georgia, Illinois, Indiana, Kentucky, Mississippi, North Carolina, Virginia

Does this spotted dog have a tail to wag? You can see the
capital of the United States in his eye. What is it?
How many states can you find?

District of Columbia. Florida, Kansas, Maryland, Missouri, Montana, Ohio,
Pennsylvania, South Carolina, Texas, Virginia, West Virginia

Here is a pretty flower growing in a
pot. Is your state here? Is it in the
blossom, the stem, or the flowerpot?

Alabama, California, Idaho, Illinois, Iowa, Kentucky,
Louisiana, New York, North Carolina, Ohio, Oregon,
Tennessee, Washington

23

Is your state going for a walk with this man and his dog?

Connecticut, Georgia, Idaho, Iowa, Kentucky, Maine, Minnesota, New Hampshire, Oklahoma, Tennessee, Vermont

24

Round and round goes this carousel horse. Is your state bobbing up and down on the merry-go-round?

Colorado, Florida, Georgia, Illinois, Indiana, Kentucky, Maryland, Nebraska, New Jersey, North Carolina, North Dakota, Oklahoma, South Dakota, Tennessee, Vermont, Wyoming

25

This clown works at the circus. Is your state there with him?
Which states are there?

Alaska, Arizona, Arkansas, California, Connecticut, Delaware, Hawaii, Idaho, Louisiana, Maine, Massachusetts, Michigan, Minnesota, Mississippi, Missouri, Montana, Nevada, New Hampshire, New Mexico, Oregon, Rhode Island, South Carolina, Utah, Virginia, West Virginia, Wisconsin

Trivia U.S.A.

1. East of the Mississippi River, which state is the largest?
2. Which state is the smallest in the U.S.A.?
3. The Mississippi River begins in what state?
4. Which state is the largest in the U.S.A.?
5. Where can you stand on four states all at once?
6. Which five states have beaches on the Gulf of Mexico?
7. Which five states have land touching the Pacific Ocean?
8. How many states touch the border of our southern neighbor, Mexico? Can you name them?
9. Which fourteen states are on the Atlantic Ocean?
10. The Mississippi River enters the Gulf of Mexico through which state?
11. Which thirteen states share a land or water border with our northern neighbor, Canada?
12. Which state has two parts, a lower peninsula and an upper peninsula?
13. The capital of the United States, the District of Columbia, is also known as Washington, D.C. Which two states does it border?

Puzzle Keys

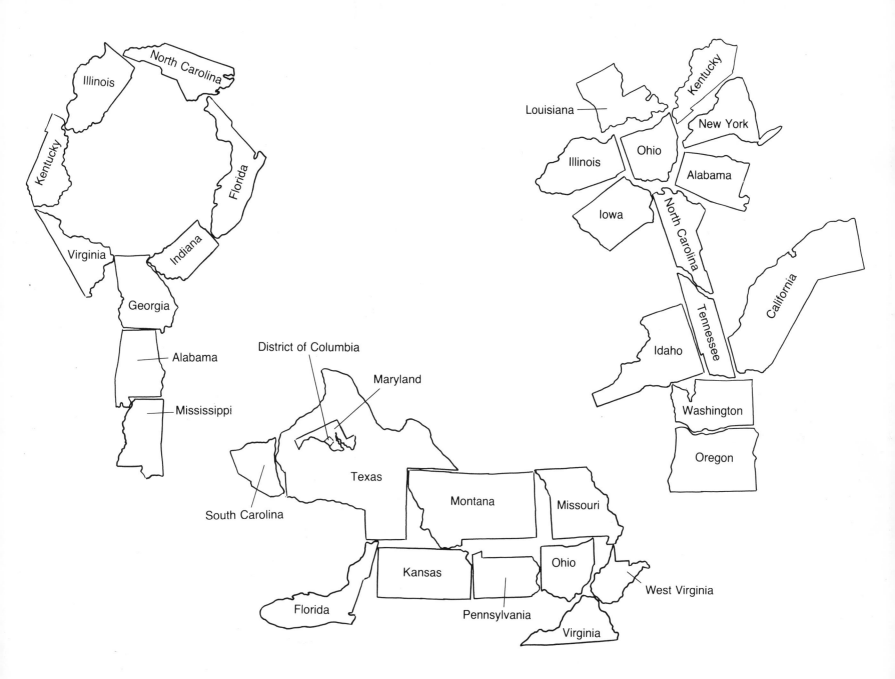

North Carolina

Illinois

Kentucky

Florida

Virginia

Indiana

Georgia

Alabama

Mississippi

Louisiana

Kentucky

New York

Ohio

Illinois

Alabama

Iowa

North Carolina

California

Tennessee

Idaho

Washington

Oregon

District of Columbia

Maryland

Texas

South Carolina

Montana

Missouri

Kansas

Ohio

West Virginia

Florida

Pennsylvania

Virginia

29

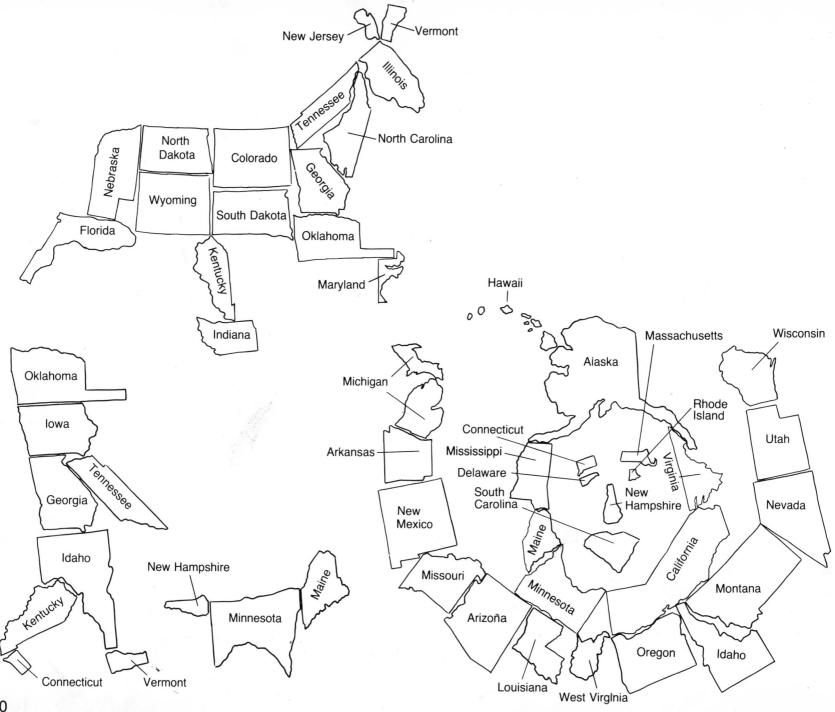

New Jersey — Vermont

Illinois

Tennessee

North Carolina

Nebraska

North Dakota

Colorado

Georgia

Wyoming

South Dakota

Florida

Kentucky

Oklahoma

Indiana

Maryland

Hawaii

Massachusetts

Wisconsin

Alaska

Michigan

Rhode Island

Connecticut

Oklahoma

Mississippi

Utah

Iowa

Delaware

Virginia

Arkansas

South Carolina

New Hampshire

Tennessee

New Mexico

Nevada

Georgia

Maine

Idaho

California

New Hampshire

Maine

Missouri

Montana

Minnesota

Kentucky

Arizona

Oregon

Idaho

Connecticut

Vermont

Minnesota

Louisiana

West Virginia

Trivia U.S.A.—Answers

1. Georgia.
2. Rhode Island.
3. Minnesota.
4. Alaska. It is so large that if a map of it were drawn to the same scale as the maps of the other states, it would be almost as big as all the other states put together.
5. Arizona, Colorado, New Mexico, Utah.
6. Alabama, Florida, Louisiana, Mississippi, Texas.
7. Alaska, California, Hawaii, Oregon, Washington.
8. Four states: Arizona, California, New Mexico, Texas.
9. Connecticut, Delaware, Florida, Georgia, Maine, Maryland, Massachusetts, New Hampshire, New Jersey, New York, North Carolina, Rhode Island, South Carolina, Virginia.
10. Louisiana
11. Alaska, Idaho, Maine, Michigan, Minnesota, Montana, North Dakota, New Hampshire, New York, Ohio, Pennsylvania, Vermont, Washington.
12. Michigan.
13. Maryland and Virginia.

Index